Ninety-nine Potcakes

Alice Bain

MACMILLAN
CARIBBEAN

Macmillan Education
Between Towns Road, Oxford OX4 3PP
A division of Macmillan Publishers Limited
Companies and representatives throughout the world

www.macmillan-caribbean.com

ISBN 978 0 333 97659 3

First published 2003

Typeset by EXPO Holdings, Malaysia
Illustrated by Lynda Knott
Cover design by AC Design
Cover illustration by Lynda Knott

Printed in Malaysia

2015 2014 2013 2012 2011
13 12 11 10 9 8 7 6 5

I live on an island, far out in the sea,
but I don't live alone — my puppy's with me.
There's just one of him and there's just
     one of me,
and that is the way that we like it to be.

But …
it wasn't always this way.

I used to be sad, as I lived all alone.
There was no one to greet me when
I arrived home.

Then one day, coming back home from
    my job,
I got out of my car and I heard a
    small sob.

And there by the door, in the shade of
   a tree,
a small frightened puppy was looking at me!

He needed a bath and he wanted a feed,
this cute little puppy that was of mixed breed.

They're mongrels in England
and mutts in the States,
but here in the Islands
we call them *potcakes*!

I bathed him and then, as he dried
    in the Sun,
I went to the store and bought food
    by the ton.

That potcake was hungry, no doubt
    about that.
He cleaned out his bowl in just two
    seconds flat!

Then we went down to the beach
and played in the Sun.
I threw him some sticks and we had lots
of fun.

I said when I went to my job the next day,
'Now be a good potcake while I am away.
Don't chew up my flip-flops and don't
    hide your bone
under the cushions or on top of the phone.'

That night I called 'Hi!' as I opened the
     door.
I heard one bark, then two — and then
     more and more!

He'd invited ten friends to stay in my yard.
'Ten dogs to look after, that will be hard.'

But I called the dogs over and fed them
    all well,
and then bathed the lot for they really
    did smell.

But …

It didn't stop there, for the very next day
each potcake brought *eight* of his friends
   round to stay.
Eleven times eight, can you work out
   that sum?
That's *eighty-eight* dogs! Where did they
   come from?

Then add in one potcake and all the first ten, that's *ninety-nine* potcakes here in my den!

I drove to the pet shop, just by myself,
and bought all the food that they had on
the shelf.

But that wasn't enough, they still wanted
   more,
so I had to drive out to another pet store.

Now I'm fond of all animals, cats, dogs
    and such,
but *ninety-nine* potcakes is simply
    too much.

I said to myself, 'Well, I can't keep them all.'
So I sat for a bit, thinking, 'Who can I call?'

I rang up two friends, I knew they'd
   work hard.
'I have ninety-nine potcakes here in
   my yard!
They all need good places that they can
   call home
and people who'll feed them and not let
   them roam.'

'I know that you'll help me, so here's what
    we'll do,
to find more people, please each call up two.
Ask each to call two more and pass the
    word on
until at last every potcake has finally gone.'

So they each called two people ...
and they called two people ...
and they called two people ...
and they called two people ...

Now how many people do you think that
    makes?
Sixty-two, if I have made no mistakes!

Sixty-two people, and when you count me to help out these potcakes, that makes sixty-three.

Some people took one dog, some people
    took two.
Every dog was adopted by the time we
    were through.

So now all those potcakes have homes of
their own,
with a bowl of clean water and a nice
meaty bone.

But Potcake the First still lives here with me
on this beautiful island, far out in the sea.

Ping Pong P-Pan Barbara Applin *0-333-74142-0*
Click! Flash! Barbara Applin *0-333-92077-5*
Water for Monique Shelley Davidow & Catherine Parrill *0-333-97429-8*
The School that Sank Sherry North *0-333-97658-4*

The Angry Mountain Claudette Megan Adams *0-333-74144-7*
Carly And The Crabholes Natalie Williams *0-333-95445-9*
The Scottish-Island Girl Joanne Gail Johnson *0-333-92991-0*
Saving Mr Omardeen Judy Stone *0-333-77623-2*
Gary The Smartest Gecko Thalia Bell *0-333-95446-7*

The Taming of Pudding Pan Berna McIntosh *0-333-74141-2*
Fisherwoman Effie Adrienne *0-333-74143-9*
Sally's Way Joanne Johnson *0-333-95450-5*
Jeremia And The Trumpet Man Petronella Breinburg *0-333-92065-1*
Running For Real Marcia François *0-333-92234-4*
Fire And Steel Judy Stone *0-333-77622-4*
Go! Krabita! Go! Petronella Breinburg *0-333-95305-3*
The Village Storyteller Claudette Megan Adams *0-333-97632-0*